D1456405

CINDY'S SNOWDROPS

Doris Orgel

CINDY'S
SNOWDROPS

illustrated by Ati Forberg

Alfred A. Knopf *New York*

THIS IS A BORZOI BOOK PUBLISHED BY ALFRED A. KNOPF, INC.

Library of Congress Catalog Card Number: AC 66-10178

For Megan Lee

"Let's go to the nursery and buy some bulbs," said Cindy's father one September day.

Cindy knew what kind of nursery. Not the one for little people. The one for little plants. And she knew what kind of bulbs. Not the bulbs you put in lamps to make light. Bulbs you put in the ground to make flowers.

The bulbs looked like onions. Cindy found some
just the right size to put in a salad for dolls.
"Snowdrops," said the nurseryman.

"It does," thought Cindy. But she knew he didn't mean snow that drops from the sky.

The snowdrop bulbs were the littlest bulbs.

Cindy was the littlest in her family. Last September, when she was still too little, all she had done was watch her parents and her brother, Gus, plant *their* bulbs. *She* hadn't planted any.

But now she picked out six snowdrop bulbs. "I'm going to plant these all by myself," she said.

The nurseryman showed her a picture. "Here's what they'll look like," he said.

"When?" asked Cindy.

"Oh, about March."

"I'll be six in March," said Cindy.

"Will you?" said the nurseryman. "Well, here's an extra one for you to grow on." And he gave her an extra bulb. He also gave her the picture of snowdrops to keep.

Cindy's father was planting
tulip bulbs in front of the house.

Cindy's mother was planting
daffodil bulbs in the moist soil
by the brook.

Her brother, Gus, was planting crocus bulbs in the
rose bed by the driveway.

"Where will you plant your snowdrop bulbs?"
asked Cindy's father.

Cindy didn't know yet. First
she had to walk all around the
garden and look at everything,
and imagine everything away,
so she could imagine what the
garden would be like—
oh, about March.

It was hard, imagining everything away, when everything was
still like summer—green and warm
and blooming. But she had to.
She imagined the leaves off the
trees. She imagined the roses
away, the zinnias and marigolds
away, the warmth away. Then she
imagined wind and cold coming, and snow—and then
snow starting to go away again.

All that took a lot of walking
around. It took a lot of
looking, and also the
kind of looking you
can only do with your
eyes closed. It took
a long time.

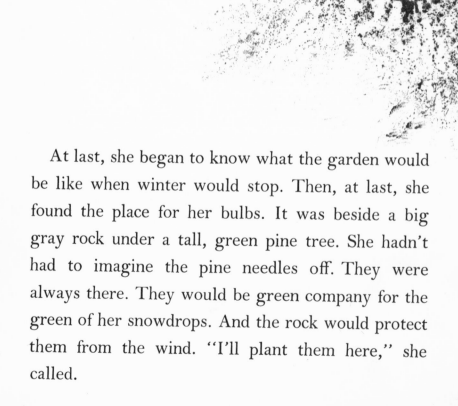

At last, she began to know what the garden would be like when winter would stop. Then, at last, she found the place for her bulbs. It was beside a big gray rock under a tall, green pine tree. She hadn't had to imagine the pine needles off. They were always there. They would be green company for the green of her snowdrops. And the rock would protect them from the wind. "I'll plant them here," she called.

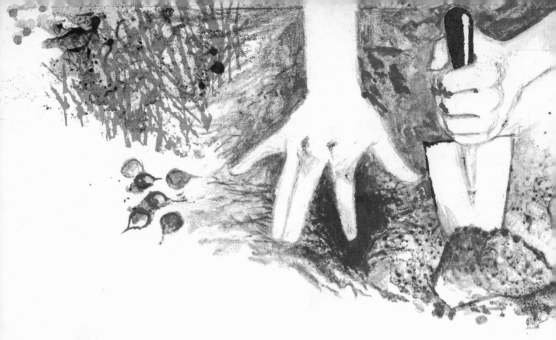

Digging here was not as easy as in the sand at the beach. Cindy no sooner started than her trowel struck something hard—a stone. She loosened the soil all around it. When she lifted it out, she came to a big brown worm making itself into waves. "Gus!" she called, "look what I found!"

She gave the worm to Gus for his collection. Then she asked her father if the hole was deep enough yet.

Her father looked. "Not yet," he said.

Cindy dug some more. She had to take out pebbles, and cut through ribbons of roots, thick and thin. She dug till the hole was even deeper than her pointing finger was long.

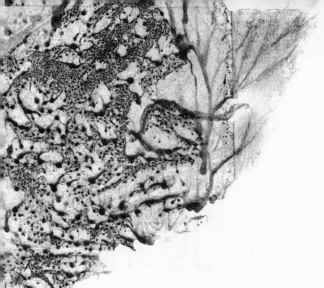

"Now it's deep enough," her father said.

Cindy put a bulb in. Gently, she covered it and filled up the hole with soil.

Meanwhile, Gus had planted all his crocus bulbs. "I'll help you dig if you'll let me have all the worms," he offered. But Cindy said no. She wanted to do it alone.

She dug and dug—two, three, four, five, six holes—going around in a circle.

"You'd better stop now, it's almost suppertime," her mother called.

But Cindy still had one more hole to dig. "Where?" she wondered. "I know! In the middle!" And that was where she planted the seventh, extra snowdrop bulb.

Before she went to sleep that night, Cindy taped
the picture of snowdrops to the wall beside her bed.

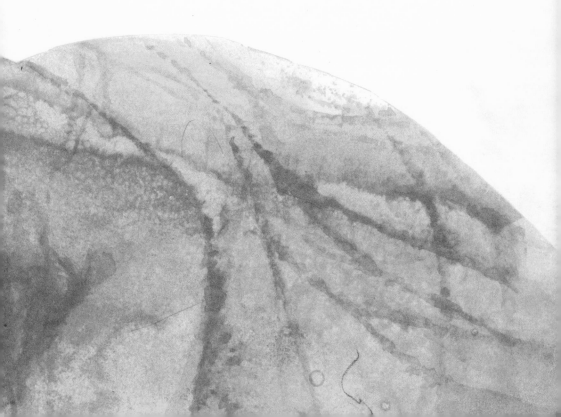

Soon it was fall.
Cindy and Gus helped rake the fallen
leaves off the lawn. They heaped them in
a corner of the driveway. When the heap
was high, they jumped on it
and rolled in it.

Then the trees were bare, only the pine tree stayed green. The brook got a sheet of crackly ice. And one morning, when Cindy looked out her window, there was no more lawn, only snow. Now there were so many winter things to do, she might have forgotten her bulbs. But the picture on the wall reminded her, and often at bedtime she thought of them sleeping, deep in the ground.

One morning, Cindy looked out her window at the gray rock sticking out of the snow by the pine tree. She made up a rhyme.

Snowdrops
when the winter stops

She told it to Gus when he woke up. He wrote it down for her. Then *he* made up a rhyme.

GUS'S
Crocusses

Cindy thought hers was better. She said it again:
"*Snowdrops*
When the winter stops."

But winter had not stopped yet, it was only February. The garden still looked like Cindy had imagined it—snowy, windy, cold—and icicles hung from the picnic table. Yet, waking up very early one morning, she saw from her window a very green something beside the gray rock. It couldn't be pine needles, it was much brighter. But maybe somebody had dropped a little bit of green paper there, and that was all it was. Or was it, could it be—

In slippers and bathrobe she ran downstairs, out the door, over the snowy lawn and—yes! There, in a bit of brown earth, stood the first spring-green stem, growing into a pointy leaf with a tiny edge of white at the top where the snowdrop bud would very soon be!

"Get inside this minute, what do you think you're doing out there?" yelled her mother from the house.

Cindy ran back in and didn't even notice her wet slippers or how cold she was. "One of my snowdrop's starting!" she shouted.

    The next day felt as if winter were stopping. Most of the snow had melted. The edge of white on Cindy's snowdrop leaf was broader and, near it, another bit of bright green was pushing up out of the ground.

    Cindy was proud and excited. She thought of her birthday, ten days from now. How wonderful if all her snowdrops would be out by then!

But snow began again that night and fell and fell.

"Hurry up, slowpoke," said Gus in the morning. "Get your sled! Everyone's sledding on Cobble Hill!"

"I'm not going," said Cindy. She thought of her poor snowdrops probably lying there all frozen underneath this cold thick blanket. "I hate the snow!" she said.

It stayed cold. The snow stayed on the ground. Cindy cried because it wouldn't go away. She stopped hoping to see her snowdrops out for her birthday—or ever.

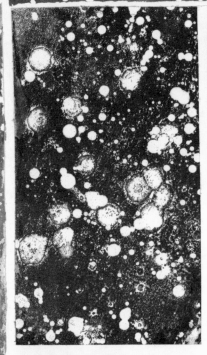

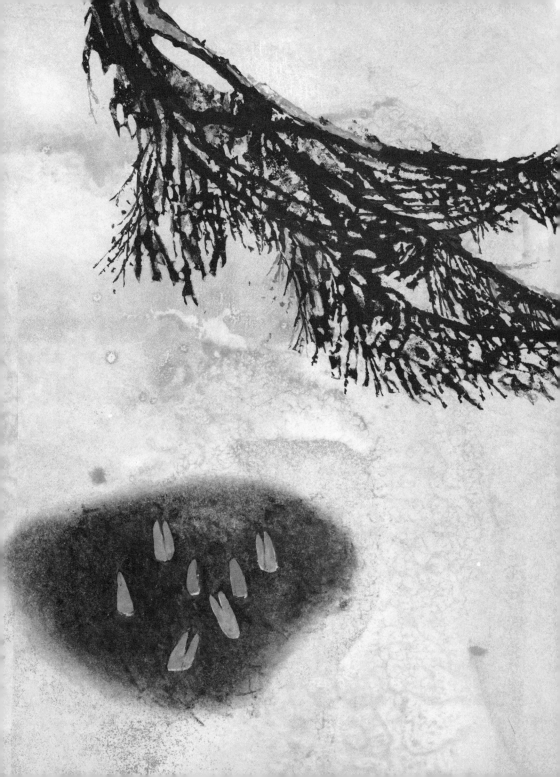

But on the third of March, her birthday morning, from her window, this is what Cindy saw:

Sunshine.

More lawn than snow.

A chickadee swinging on a twig of the pine tree.

And, under the tree, a circle of earth, brown as a chocolate cake. And standing all around that circle, six bright green somethings that were *not* bits of paper, and a seventh, extra one to grow on, in the middle.

Faster than the last time,
Cindy ran downstairs again,
out again, and over to the seven
somethings—her snowdrops!
They hadn't minded the snow at all.
No, they had thrived and grown in it,
and now three of them were open
little bells. Three were buds,
and one was still only a leaf
with a promise of white
at the tip.

This time Cindy's mother did not yell. Instead, when Cindy came back inside, her mother sang to her. So did her father and Gus. They all sang *Happy Birthday*.

And on the kitchen table stood a cake—dark brown, chocolate—with six green candles around it, and one in the middle to grow on.

Cindy blew the candles out. Then she and Gus and their mother and father ate the cake up for breakfast—why not?

But Cindy's snowdrops stayed a long time. Two of them were still in bloom when the first of Gus's crocusses came up, a whole month later.

Text is set in Bell. Composed at Westcott & Thomson, Philadelphia, Pennsylvania. Printed by Polygraphic Company of America, Inc., New York, New York. Bound by Economy Bookbinding Corporation, Kearny, New Jersey. Typography by Atha Tehon.